To Heidi,
with love from Mummy xxx

M.R.

To my sister Jessica,
who has a wonderful smile xx

B.M.S.

WALKER BOOKS
AND SUBSIDIARIES
LONDON • BOSTON • SYDNEY • AUCKLAND

First published 2019 by Walker Books Ltd, 87 Vauxhall Walk, London SE11 5HJ • This edition published 2020 • Text © 2019 Michelle Robinson • Illustrations © 2019 Briony May Smith • The right of Michelle Robinson and Briony May Smith to be identified as author and illustrator of this work respectively has been asserted by them in accordance with the Copyright, Designs and Patents Act 1988 This book has been typeset in Walbaum • Printed in China • All rights reserved. No part of this book may be reproduced, transmitted or stored in an information retrieval system in any form or by any means, graphic, electronic or mechanical, including photocopying, taping and recording, without prior written permission from the publisher • British Library Cataloguing in Publication Data: a catalogue record for this book is available from the British Library • ISBN 978-1-4063-9095-7 • www.walker.co.uk • 10 9 8 7 6 5 4 3 2 1

This Walker book belongs to:

by

TOOTH FAIRY
in Training

Michelle Robinson

illustrated by

Briony May Smith

My Tooth Fairy training starts today!
I'm learning from my sister, May.

May says, "*First thing fairies do is practise the old switcheroo.*

*Lift the pillow,
look beneath …*

leave the coins …

and take the teeth.

*Do it well and
you're a keeper.*

*One rule, Tate:
don't wake the sleeper."*

So I go gently.

Piece of cake!

May says,
"Now do it …

in a lake."

This baby hippo
needs a visit.

Not every child's a
human, is it?

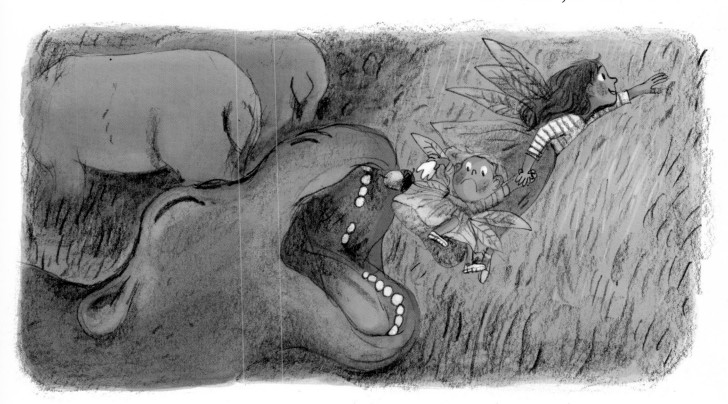

*"Careful," May says, "some kids bite.
Quick, Tate, we haven't got all night!"*

I dry my wings
for visit two.

May says, "Not the kangaroo.

Your next tooth's waiting down that trail…"

I duck and dodge the mother's tail.

"Come on!" May says…

And down we go. She gurgles, *"Mind the undertow!"*

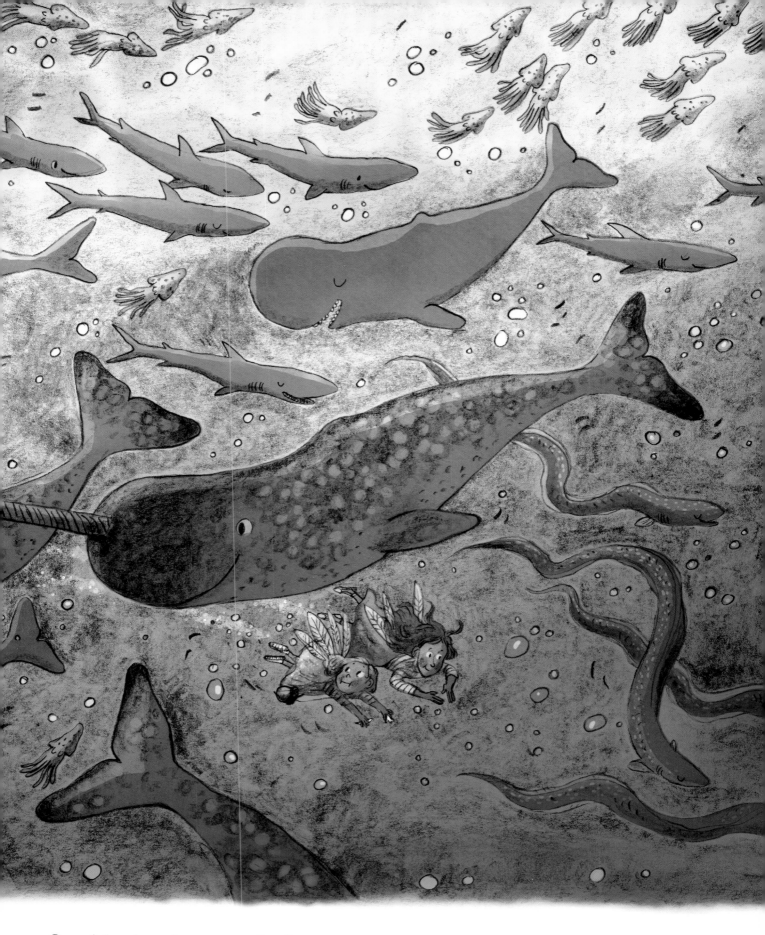

Squid, shark, narwhal, conger eel. *"Up next,"* May says…

"A fluffy seal."

I ask, *"This one?"* May says, *"The other."*

Oh dear — I think she means its brother.

It can't get worse than *that* now, can it?
We've almost done the entire *planet*.

Just a gentle
jungle wander ...

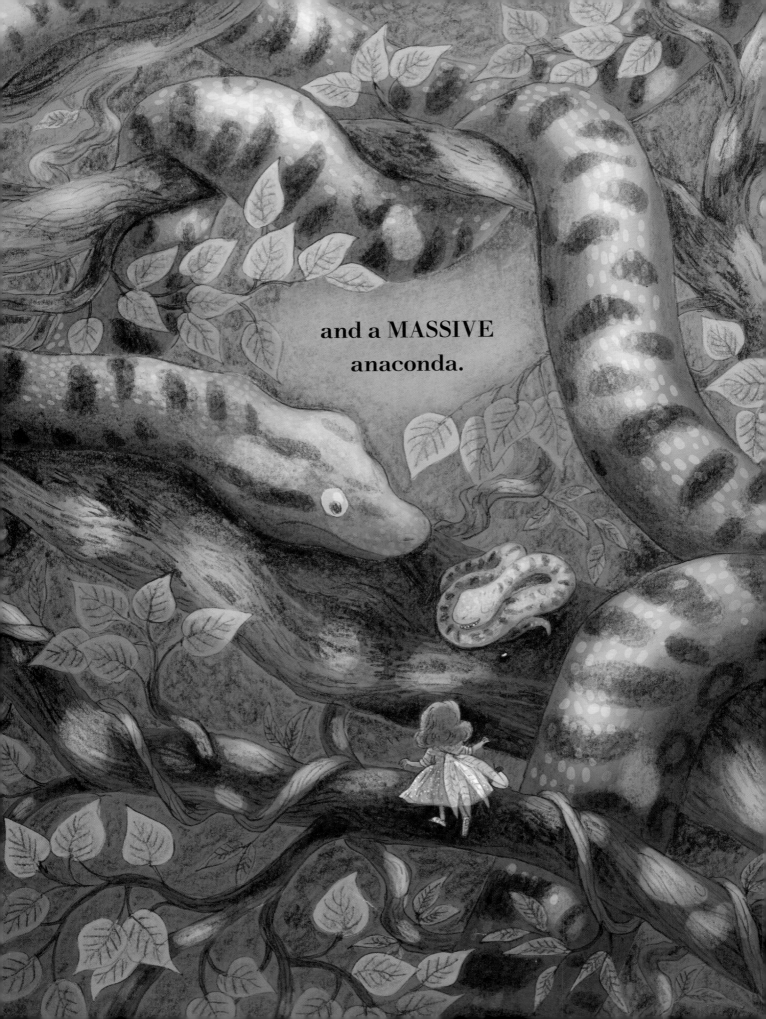

and a MASSIVE
anaconda.

Snakes lose teeth as well,
you know.

"And swallow fairies,"
May says. "GO!

Well done, Tate.
Snake teeth are rare.

One final tooth then
home, I swear."

A little girl.
I can't go wrong.

But hang on —
where's my money gone?

CLANG!

Oh no! She's woken! OW!

May says, *"We're in big trouble now!"*

Of all the teeth!
Of all the kids!
The sharks! The crocs!
The giant squids!

I had to get caught
by *Melissa* ...
doll-collecting,
fairy kisser.

I flap my wings. I make a wish.

I give my magic wand a SWISH!

Before Melissa knows what's hit her …
I've covered her in sleepy glitter.

Home at last, May's proud of me.
"You did it by yourself." Yippee!
Tooth Fairy Tate! I passed the test!
But even *fairies* need their rest.

It's lights-out time in Fairy Town.

May whispers as I snuggle down,
*"We'll fetch more teeth tomorrow night—
Melissa lost one more. Sleep tight!"*

Michelle Robinson previously wrote copy for some of the world's biggest brands. Now she is either busy writing stories or busy sharing them with children at events across the UK. Her picture books include *How to Wash a Woolly Mammoth*, illustrated by Kate Hindley, *There's a Lion in My Cornflakes*, illustrated by Jim Field, and *A Beginner's Guide to Bear Spotting*, illustrated by David Roberts. Michelle lives in Frome with her husband, son and daughter. Find Michelle online at michellerobinson.co.uk, and on Twitter and Instagram as @MicheRobinson.

Briony May Smith graduated from Falmouth University with a First Class degree in Illustration. Since then, she has been shortlisted for the British Comic Awards and has twice been highly commended for the Macmillan Children's Prize. She is the author-illustrator of *Imelda and the Goblin King*, and the illustrator of *The Giant's Necklace*, written by Michael Morpurgo. She is inspired by traditional fairy tales and folklore, and by the surrounding countryside of her home in Devon. Find her online at brionymaysmith.com and on Twitter and Instagram as @BrionyMaySmith.